# 21st Century Quiz

# 21st Century Quiz

Anita Kaul

Srishti Publishers & Distributors
Registered Office: N-16, C.R. Park
New Delhi – 110 019
Corporate Office: 212A, Peacock Lane
Shahpur Jat, New Delhi – 110 049
editorial@srishtipublishers.com

First published by SRISHTI PUBLISHERS & DISTRIBUTORS in 2002
Copyright © Srishti Publishers & Distributors

ISBN 81-87075-94-5

Cover design by Vinayak Contemporary Painter

All rights reserved. No part of this publication may
be reproduced, stored in a retrieval system, or transmitted,
in any form or by any means, electronic, mechanical,
photocopying, recording or otherwise,
without the prior written permission of the Publishers.

# Contents

Introduction

Art and Culture | 1

Religion | 23

Literature | 37

History | 45

Science | 73

Sports | 113

Miscellaneous | 137

# Introduction

Quizzes and quzzing are fun, competitive and a way of gathering knowledge all packed into one. To keep the interest and entertainment value intact all through this collection, we have ensured that the questions evoke interest as well as impart knowledge. The questions are therefore derived from general knowledge rather than from specialised works.

The questions are all accompanied with answers at the end of the collection so that the reader may try to answer them on their own at first in keeping with the spirit of quizzes. A variety of facts have been sourced, aiming at directing the interest of the reader to different fields and subjects. Consequently the questions have been grouped into a number of sections namely, Cultural Heritage, under which comes Art, Culture, Literature, and Religion; History; Science; Sports and Miscellaneous.

This collection has tried to bring into focus facts which are an integral part of human evolution and cultural and scientific developments in human society as well as the curious facts about the rest of the world around us, both living and non-living. Competitions and quiz games based on these facts may be developed by the readers fulfilling the objective of the book in a broader perspective.

# Questions
## Art and Culture

1. Rajput miniature paintings of music are known by a name. What is it?

2. Which is the birthplace of the Kangra School of Art?

3. One Mughal Emperor invited Persian painters Mir Sayad Ali and Abdus Samad to his court. Who was he?

4. Fine metal inlay known as Bidri work flourished in which place in South India?

5. A legend says these artisans of Madhya Pradesh were cursed to work only with lac and glass after their ancestors were believed to have helped the Kauravas to build the lac palace. Name the community.

6. What is the Jaipuri skill of inlaying delicate fillets of copper in wood called?

7. An Indian fabric was used for wrapping mummies in Ancient Egypt. What was it?

8. When a weaver began to weave for a king, a gun salute was fired. This happened in which state?

9. A Jamavar shawl is a paisley shawl originally woven in this part of India. Name the place.

10. What are Kanchipuram weavers called?

11. The Bohra community of Jamnagar is specially skilled in this craft. What is the craft?

12. What is the name given to a type of devotional group singing of Kashmir which is close to the music of Central Asia?

13. In Indian music, a melodic scheme of 10 characteristics is supposed to be the precursor of the *raga*. What is it called?

14. The *Tillana* of Bharatanatyam and *Tarana* of Kathak is similar to this step of Odissi dance. What is the name given to it?

15. In Hindustani and Carnatic systems of music some ragas have identical music arrangements. Rag Yaman is similar to which raga of Carnatic music?

16. Who was the first woman sarod player and the first instrumentalist to receive the Padmashri?

17. Name the first Indian film in English directed by Ezra Mir.

18. Which actor has played the role of a police officer in more than 150 films?

19. Name the first Hollywood film to be dubbed in Hindi.

20. Which Indian magician is the only one to have been honoured with a Padmashri?

21. Name the poetess who was the first woman to contest elections?

22. India has the largest number of languages in the world. How many?

23. Uday Shankar made only one film which was based on the theme of dance. Name it.

24. Which film personality was recently kidnapped and held captive in the jungles for nearly 2 months?

25. With an improvement on the Veena, he invented the sitar. Name the person.

26. In ancient times, North India was called by a different name. What was it?

27. Derived from the Persian word for spectacle, this form of entertainment flourished during the Maratha period. What form of dance is it?

28. Who is called the father of Indian Carnatic music or Karnataka Sangeet Pitamaha?

29. This 432-km long road is the world's highest road. Name it.

30. Pashmina wool is obtained from a mountain. Where is it found in India?

31. Ghoomar is a folk dance of this state. Name the state.

32. A classical dance form of India is based on the life story of Lord Krishna. Name the dance form.

33. One daughter of Mughal Emperor Aurangzeb wrote mystical poems in which she tried to fuse elements of Hinduism, Islam and Zoroastrianism. Name her.

34. Which was the first all-woman film in which there were no male characters?

35. Which film featured Sanjeev Kumar in 9 different roles?

36. The first talkie of India was *Alam Ara*. Who was the heroine of the film?

37. The film *Ek Chadar Maile Se* was based on whose novel by the same name?

## ART AND CULTURE

38. *Vogue* magazine once described this Indian actress as one of the five most beautiful women. Who was the lady?

39. Who has won the maximum number of Filmfare Awards so far?

40. Where is India's first Multiplex located?

41. The film *Mughaloe-Azam* was a blockbuster. Who composed the music for the film?

42. Which Indian actress kissed Prince Charles on his first visit to India?

43. In 1982, the first Sanskrit film was screened. Name it.

44. Who was the first Indian Music Director for foreign films?

45. Who was the first Indian musician to conduct the London Philharmonic Orchestra?

46. Who is the Music Director with whom Lata Mangeshkar never worked?

47. A sari with a double-colour border was made popular after this film. Name it.

48. Which was India's first film regarded as a box office hit.

49. Name the only film with 71 songs in it.

50. The Samarth family has given three generations of film actresses to the film world. Name the youngest member of the family.

51. The biggest scroll painting bearing the image of Guru Padma Sambhava is four storeys high. Where was it unscrolled in 1992?

52. Who was the first recipient of the Dada Sahib Phalke Award in 1969?

53. Name the first film of Amitabh Bachchan's son Abhishek.

54. Name the longest running film which ran for nearly six years in Bombay.

ART AND CULTURE

55. Who was the woman behind the construction of Chandini Chowk in Delhi?

56. Where was the first woman's University started in 1916?

57. Pandit Jasraj, an eminent 20<sup>th</sup> century Hindustani vocalist is from this Gharana. Name the Gharana.

58. Name the Indian film star whose wax statue stands at Madam Tussaud's in London.

59. Which Indian film director received the highest number (four) of awards for the best director?

60. Who won the first ever National Award for Best Actress for her last film?

61. What were the Film Fare awards called earlier?

62. The highest award in Indian cinema is named after this person. Name him.

63. Which country gives the Magsaysay Awards?

64. The Jnanpith Award is given for which profession?

65. Which was Munshi Premchand's first published novel?

66. Who is the ruler in the book *Alice in Wonderland*?

67. Name the actress who is the daughter of renowned artist Jatin Das.

68. Who is regarded as the father of Tamil literature?

69. Whose first novel was *Swami and His Father*?

70. Who wrote the book *Politics*?

71. Sangam literature is associated with which state?

72. The Sahitya Akademi Awards are given to people who have excelled in this field.

73. Name the author of *Das Capital*.

74. Who is known as the 'bard of Avon'?

75. *Satanic Verses* is banned in India. Who wrote this book?

76. Which country has won the maximum number of Nobel Prizes for Literature?

77. Which language is considered the mother of all languages?

78. The statue of *Gomateswara*, a Jain sage, is the tallest monolithic statue in the world. Where is it located?

79. Which country depicts the Ramayana in a dance form?

80. In which Veda is the theory of classical music described?

81. Which is regarded as the oldest Dravidian language?

82. Shiv Kumar Sharma is associated with which musical instrument?

83. Patta paintings are done on rugged, rough cloth. This is a traditional art of which state?

84. On which river is the city of Mathura located?

85. According to Greek mythology, which was the first wonder of the world?

86. Which zodiac sign is denoted by the bull?

87. Which state is the 'milk pail' of India?

88. Who in Greek mythology is a mythical monster that was half-serpent and half-woman?

89. Who is the Goddess of Youth in Roman mythology?

90. How many *Chakras* are there in the body that can be worked out by Yoga?

91. Who was responsible for a great religious revival in Bengal?

92. Which song was so liked by singer K. L. Saigal that it was even played at his funeral?

93. Which was the first black and white film to be converted to colour?

94. Who is the only Indian actress to have been honoured with a retrospective of her films in Paris?

ART AND CULTURE

95. Who holds the record for acting in the highest number of films (100)?

96. Which artist was so inspired by actress Madhuri Dixit that he made a film with her?

97. In which Bond film does Vijay Amritraj say "Game, set, match" after eluding his villainous pursuers?

98. Which Indian athlete starred in a semi-autobiographical film named after her?

99. Which star politician acted in over 40 mythological films?

100. Which Indian actress changed her name to Begum Ayesha Sultana after her marriage?

101. This famous actress was known as Mahajabeen Alibux before her entry into films. Who was she?

102. Which English architect made the layout for the city of New Delhi?

103. What are the gardens at Rashtrapati Bhawan called?

104. Every year a kite festival is held in Ahmedabad? What is it called?

105. Where in India will you find the Vivekanda Rock?

106. Only one temple in the world is dedicated to Lord Brahma, the creator of the Universe. Where is it?

107. Kathakali is associated with which Indian state?

108. The National Museum at Delhi has some antique collections. How old is the oldest relic found here?

109. Which 1000-year-old monastery in Himachal Pradesh is called the "Ajanta of the Himalayas"?

110. This festival of Ladakh is famous for its colourful mask dances. Name it.

# Answers
## Art and Culture

1. Raagmala
2. Guler
3. Humayun
4. Bidar, Andhra Pradesh
5. Lakheras
6. Tarqakshi
7. Mulmul Khas
8. Manipur
9. Kashmir
10. Salgars

11. Intricate crocheted lace caps.

12. Sufiyana Kalaam

13. The Jati

14. Tarajan

15. Raga Kalyani

16. Sharan Rani

17. Noor Jahan

18. Jagdish Raj

19. Jurassic Park

20. P. C. Sorkar

21. Kamaladevi Chattopadhayaya

22. 845 languages

23. Kalpana

24. Raj Kumar

25. Amir Khusro
26. Uttaravart
27. Tamasha
28. Purandaradasa
29. Srinagar-Leh Road
30. Ladakh
31. Rajasthan
32. Manipuri
33. Zebunissa Makhfi
34. Rukmabai Ki Haveli
35. Naya Din Naye Raat
36. Zubeida
37. Rajinder Singh Bedi
38. Leela Naidu

39. Kamalahasan

40. Chennai

41. Naushad

42. Padmini Kolaphure

43. Shankaracharya

44. Ravi Shankar

45. Naushad

46. O. P. Nayyar

47. Ganga Jamuna

48. Chandralekha

49. Indrasabha

50. Kajol

51. Hemis Gumpa, Ladakh, J& K

52. Devika Rani

ART AND CULTURE

53. Refugee

54. Sholay

55. Jehanara Begum, daughter of Shah Jahan

56. Pune

57. Gwalior Gharana

58. Amitabh Bachchan

59. Satyajit Ray

60. Nargis

61. Clares

62. Dada Saheb Phalke

63. Philippines

64. Literature

65. Sansar Ka Anmol Ratna

66. The Queen of Hearts

67. Nandita Das

68. Swami Agastya

69. R. K. Narayan

70. Aristotle

71. Tamil Nadu

72. Literature

73. Karl Marx

74. Shakespeare

75. Salman Rushdie

76. France

77. Sanskrit

78. Karnataka

79. Indonesia

80. Sam Veda

## ART AND CULTURE

81. Tamil

82. Santoor

83. Orissa

84. Yamuna

85. Pyramids

86. Taurus

87. Haryana

88. Delphyne

89. Juventas

90. 7

91. Chaitanya

92. Jab dil hi toot Gaya

93. Yankee Doodle Dandy

94. Smita Patil

95. Manorama

96. M. F. Husain

97. Octupussy

98. Ashwini Nachappa

99. N. T. Rama Rao

100. Sharmila Tagore

101. Meena Kumari

102. Edwin Lutyens

103. Mughal Gardens

104. Uttarayan

105. Kanyakumari

106. Pushkar in Rajasthan

107. Kerala

108. 5000-year-old-relics of the Indus Valley civilisation

ART AND CULTURE

109. Tabo in Spiti valley

110. Hemis festival

# Questions
## Religion

1. Subhadara was the mother of which warrior prince?

2. Whose mother was Hidimba?

3. In which part of Maharashtra is the Kumbh Mela held once in 12 years?

4. How many threads constitute the sacred thread (Yagnopavit) of Brahmins?

5. The blue lotus is an emblem of this hero of Hindu mythology. Name him?

6. The oldest synagogue in the Commonwealth - the Pardesi, was built in India in 1568. Where is it located?

7. In the Roman Catholic College of Cardinals at

RELIGION

Rome, two Cardinals represent India. They are always from these two cities. Name the cities.

8. Legends say Goddess Saraswati lost her eyes here. Name this North Indian hill station which is surrounded by lakes?

9. Who bought Christianity to India?

10. The largest mosque in India was built by Shah Jahan. Name it.

11. Which is India's largest church which was built in 1652?

12. Where is the first Bahai House of Worship located?

13. The brides of this Christian community wear a mangalsutra with gold dotted cross. Name the community.

14. Muharram falls in the first month of the Hijri calendar. What does it mean?

15. Rats are worshipped in this temple which is swarming with rats. Where is it located?

16. Name the youngest religion in the country which means the "the disciple".

17. Who has translated the holy Quran into Marathi (both in prose and verse)?

18. Who was the first Jesuit missionary in India?

19. Which Kaurva Prince shifted allegiance to the Pandavas before the Mahabharata war began?

20. Name the Muslim saint who is also known as the special protector of children.

21. *Dhamal kudna*, or 'leap of virtue' over hot coals is performed by fakirs in a Muslim shrine in Uttar Pradesh. Name the shrine.

22. Both Hindus and Muslims visit a Muslim shrine at Thanjavur the city of Hindu temples. Name the shrine.

23. In which Buddhist chronicle do we find the teachings of Buddha as written down by his disciples?

RELIGION

24. Name Buddha's personal physician.

25. To which sect does the Kedarnath shrine belong?

26. Which name of Mahadevi the Hindu goddess describes the attribute 'mountain born'?

27. Who killed Dronacharaya in the battle of Kurukshetra?

28. How was Krishna related to Yudhisthra?

29. How many verses will you find in the holy *Bhagawad Gita* of the Hindus?

30. According to Indian Astrology, which planet is believed to be at the centre of the universe?

31. What was the name of Rama's fabled bow?

32. In Hindu mythology, which warrior was born with '*Kundalas*' and "*Kavacha*"?

33. The feathers of this bird always adorned the crown of Lord Krishna. Name the bird.

34. Which sage always recited '*Narayan, Narayan*' in the Mahabharata?

35. Which Demi God is Lord of Rain and Light according to Hindu mythology?

36. According to the Hindu calendar, how many days are there in a month?

37. Which *Maharishi* is believed to have created the Gayatri Mantra?

38. In Judaism, what is the collective name given to the five books of Moses that contain God's words?

39. Who wrote the Ten Commandments in Jewish scriptures?

40. When was the Church divided into two main parts – Roman Church and Eastern Orthodox Church?

41. What is the office of the Pope called?

42. Who is the God of Wine for the Romans and Greeks?

RELIGION

43. Name the 10th Guru of the Sikhs.

44. Besides Hinduism, which religious beliefs are included in Sikhism?

45. Which Christian festival falls seven Sundays after Easter?

46. This temple is called the 'Black Pagoda'. Name it.

47. What are the two sects of Islam called?

48. Which angel is believed to have appeared before Prophet Mohammad in order to give him God's message for mankind?

49. For Muslims, which is the most sacred shrine in Mecca?

50. Which hill was lifted by Lord Krishna to save the people of Vrindavan from a thunderstorm?

51. Which festival is celebrated on Prophet Mohammad's birthday?

52. The colourful festival of Orissa is the Rath Yatra

where thousands of devotees move Lord Jagannath's chariot. What is the chariot called?

53. Which is the richest Hindu temple in the world?

54. This is one of the most revered Hindu shrines in North India which is reached after a mountainous trek of 13 kms.

55. The Kumbh mela was held in Allahabad in 2001. The next Mela will be held after how many years?

56. With which dynasty are the temples of Khajuraho associated?

57. The tomb of Salim Chisti in Agra is visited by hundreds of pilgrims each year. The Samadhi of another religious leader is located here. Name the sect.

58. Where is the Bodhi tree under which Lord Buddha attained enlightenment?

59. Where is the annual Amarnath Yatra held in India?

# RELIGION

60. Which ancient temple in India is believed to be built of Gold by Somraj, the Moon God?

# Answers
## Religion

1. Abhimanayu

2. Ghatokacha

3. Nasik

4. Three

5. Karna, elder brother of Arjuna

6. Cochin, Kerala

7. Mumbai and Ernakalum

8. Nainital

9. St. Thomas

10. The Jama Masjid, Delhi

11. The Se Cathedral in Goa

12. Delhi

13. Syrian Christian community of Kerala

14. It literally means both sacred and that which is forbidden

15. Karni Mata Temple, Bikaner, Rajasthan

16. Sikhism

17. M. A. Dalvi

18. St. Francis Xavier

19. Yuyutsu, half brother of Duryodhana.

20. Shah Madar

21. At Shah Madar's tomb in Makanpur

22. The shrine of Quadinwali Sahib at Nagore.

23. The Dhammapada

24. Jivika

25. Shaivite

26. Adrija

27. Dhrishtadyumna

28. Maternal Cousin

29. 700

30. Earth

31. Kodanda

32. Karna

33. Peacock

34. Narad

35. Indra

36. 28

37. Vishwamitra

38. Torah

RELIGION

39. Moses

40. 1053

41. Papacy

42. Bacchus

43. Guru Gobind Singh

44. Islam

45. Whitsun

46. Konark temple in Orissa

47. Shia and Sunni

48. Gabriel

49. Kaaba

50. Govardhan Hill

51. Id-ul-Fitr

52. Nandighosha

53. Lord Venkateshwara temple, Tirupati

54. Vaishno Devi Shrine in Jammu.

55. 12 years

56. Chandela dynasty

57. Radhaswami

58. Bodh Gaya

59. Jammu & Kashmir

60. Somnath, Gujarat

# Questions
## Literature

1. The first modern Indian novel in English Rajmohan's wife was written by whom?

2. Who wrote Krishna Geeta in Sanskrit?

3. Which is the first feminist publishing house started by Urvashi Butalia and Ritu Menon?

4. Which South Indian language has no script of its own but is written in Kannada?

5. What was the Harappan script known as?

6. When the Ahom Kings of Burma came to rule Assam in the 16$^{th}$ century, they introduced a prose form. What is this classical Assamese literature called?

7. A saint poetess of Kashmir was famous for her four

LITERATURE

line poems which was a blend of Sufi and Shaivite philosophy. Name her.

8. The first modern Indian play was performed publicly in Calcutta. What was it called?

9. Rabindranath Tagore wrote his *Vaihanava Padabali* under a pseudonym. What was it?

10. The *Panchatantra* stories were originally devised for educating five stupid princes. Who wrote the book?

11. The oldest Modern Theatre building in India was built by the British in Shimla. What is the name of the famous theatre?

12. Who is the author of the famous book *Yama*?

13. Amitabh Bachachan is the son of a famous Hindi poet. Name him?

14. Who wrote the novel *Lajja*?

15. *Pakistan Cut to Size*. Who was the author of this book?

16. Who wrote the biography of Mahatma Gandhi?

17. Heer Ranjha is a Punjabi folklore. Who wrote it?

18. Who is the author of *Spirit of Islam*?

19. Which book did Subhash Chandra Bose write?

20. Who won the Putlitzer Prize for Literature in 2000?

21. This state of India boasts of over 200 m long suspension bridges made of cane. Name the state.

22. The Indian Lunar calendar adds a leap month in order to tally with the solar calendar. After what interval is a month added?

23. Vikram Seth was the first Indian to write an opera which had a world premiere in UK. What was the name of the opera.

24. In the 7$^{th}$ century AD which city became the centre for literature in Tamil Nadu after Madurai?

LITERATURE

25. What was the Indian dialect used by the medieval Indian poet Vidyapati?

26. What was the pen name used by the Indian composer Nyamat Shah as a personal signature in his song?

27. The 12th century text, the *Madala Panji*, or *Drum Chronicle*, tells the history of this major Indian temple? Name it.

28. A daughter of Zoroastrian elements. Who was she?

29. What is the name of the play written by Kalidasa which is the love story of a king and his court dancer?

30. Who was the first Indian to win the Booker Prize for Literature?

# Answers
## Literature

1. Bankim Chandra Chattopadhyaya

2. Manaveda Raja

3. Kali for Women

4. Tulu

5. Pictographic script

6. Buranjis

7. Lalleshwari or Lal Ded

8. Neel Darpan

9. Bhanu Sinha

10. Vishnu Sharman

11. Gaiety Theatre

LITERATURE

12. Mahadevi Verma

13. Harvansh Rai Bachchan

14. Taslima Nasreen

15. D. R. Mankekar

16. Louis Fischer

17. Warris Shah

18. Syed Ameer Ali

19. The Indian Struggle

20. Jhumpa Lahiri

21. Mizoram

22. After every 30 months

23. Arion and the Dolphin

24. Thanjavur

25. Maithili

26. Sadarang

27. Puri Jagannath temple

28. Zebunissa

29. Malavikagnimitra

30. Arundati Roy

# Questions
## History

1. There are two Ashokan pillars of the 3$^{rd}$ century BC which stand even today. One is at Lauriya Nandangarh, where is the other?

2. What is the literal meaning of Sanskrit?

3. Kashmiri is today written in Urdu. What was the original script of Kashmiri?

4. Dance Shastra, a treatise on Dance was written by which sage?

5. What word in the Puranas describes the modern day Kashmir?

6. Wajad Ali Shah, the Nawab of Lucknow composed and played a lead in this opera. Name it.

7. An Ancient Indian Emperor kept beautiful

women as his bodyguards and attendants. Who was he?

8. Which important Hindu scripture was rewritten in contemporary Sanskrit during the reign of the Guptas?

9. A series of important cave paintings were executed during the Gupta period. Name them.

10. Which Mughal Viceroy founded the independent kingdom of Deccan in the 18th century?

11. The seven sacred rivers of India are known by a word. What is it?

12. This area was originally a vast lake drained by sage Kashyapa. What is the name of this region?

13. The first Ashram which Gandhiji founded was in Durban South Africa. What was its name?

14. Which line demarcates India and Pakistan?

15. Which national leader was the first to feature on a stamp?

16. Who established the first public school for girls in India in 1943?

17. Who was the first person to speak in Hindi at the UN in 1997?

18. Which commemorative monument in India carries the maximum number of names of soldiers who died fighting?

19. Name the poetess who was the first woman to contest elections.

20. The British classified this tribe as criminal, but they were once the guardians of the Jaipur Treasury. Name the tribe.

21. The only palace facade built onto a wall of the main palace compound, is a symbol of this city. Name it.

22. This fort is lost in the mists of time and is regarded the oldest fort of the country. Name it.

3. The Maharaja of Jaipur had a pair of silver jugs made to store 8182 litres of drinking water when

HISTORY

he visited Britain. Today these are the world's largest silver articles. Where are they at present?

24. This 2,500-year-old stupa is considered the oldest building of India. Where is it located?

25. Where is the world's oldest Dockyard located?

26. These musical pillars depict different musical instruments and when struck with a stone or stick, they emit the same sound as of the instrument carved. Where can the pillars be seen?

27. The longest corridor of the world is 4002 m and is inside a temple. Name it.

28. The largest kitchen in the world has 752 ovens and over 100 varieties of food are cooked here every day. Where is it?

29. Who was the first woman to address the Congress Session in Calcutta in 1901?

30. Who was India's only Interim President?

31. Who was the only Hindu in the Muslim League in the Interim Government?

32. What is the source of the largest river in India?

33. Which Mughal Emperor created history for minting the largest coins in gold?

34. This holy city of India is believed to be older than Babylon or Mohenjo-daro. Name it.

35. This dome is second only in dimension to the St Peter's in Rome. Name it.

36. Who was the first woman ruler of the Delhi Sultanate?

37. Which Governor-General was responsible for Sati Abolition Act in India in 1829?

38. When was Vande Mataram first reported to have been used as a national call?

39. When did women get the right to sit in the Legislative Council?

40. Name the first Woman Congress President in 1917.

41. Where was the first Woman's University started in 1916?

42. Who led the first delegation of women which pushed for female franchise?

43. The daughter of Mughal Emperor Babur wrote the Humayun Nama. Name her.

44. Name the Sikh bodyguard who assassinated Indira Gandhi.

45. Who was responsible for construction of the observatories at Delhi, Jaipur, Varanasi, Mathura and Ujjain?

46. The Thousand Pillared Temple of Kakatiya dynasty is located here. Name the city.

47. This state capital's name is derived from a word which means 'Boiled beans'. Name it.

48. This fort of Rajashthan is called the sleeping beauty of Rajasthan. Name it.

49. Hyderabad was not always the capital of Andhra Pradesh. Which was the earlier capital?

50. Name the youngest state of India?

51. In the history of India, which is recorded as the worst industrial disaster?

52. The first oil pipeline was commissioned in India in 1962. Name the place.

53. Where is India's largest oilfield?

54. Where is the country's oldest export processing zone?

55. Where in India was the first oil well sunk in 1890?

56. Who issued the largest known government coin which weighs over 70 ounces?

57. Where was the first English Mint established in India in 1671?

58. Where is the palace with a thousand doors?

HISTORY

59. Which Mughal Emperor's grave is outside India?

60. Who was the only Prime Minister whose grandfather and mother also sat on the same chair?

61. Name the first couple in the Lok Sabha.

62. Who was the first non-white to become a member of the British House of Commons?

63. The Phoolwalon ki Sair is an annual fair held at the Qutub Minar in Delhi. It is held at whose grave?

64. The first Chief Minister to marry in office belonged to one of the states of the North East. Name him.

65. Who is the only former Chief Minister who was jailed while his wife was the ruling Chief Minister?

66. Who was the Prime Minister of Britain at the time of our Independence in 1947?

67. *Raghupati Raghav Raja Ram* is the famous song sung during the Dandi March of Mahatma Gandhi. Who sang it?

68. Who first coined the word 'Hindu' as a reference to people of Hindustan (India)?

69. Ashoka is generally referred to by this name in some of the inscriptions discovered.

70. Who was the Vice President of the interm government formed in 1946?

71. Which Mughal ruler remained in the captivity of his son?

72. The Indian subcontinent was originally a part of a huge landmass. What was it called?

73. Who first advocated the concept of *Anuvrata*?

74. Who first coined the word *Adivasi* to refer to tribal people?

75. Name the famous jurist of medieval India.

76. Where is the controversial Gyana Vapi Mosque built by Aurangzeb located?

HISTORY

77. Which Sikh Guru was tortured and killed on the directions of Aurangzeb?

78. Who pioneered the Extremist Party within the Congress Party?

79. Name the revolutionary who died in jail while on a hunger strike?

80. Which Governor-General took the decision to impart English education through the medium of the English language?

81. When was Mt Everest first scaled?

82. Who was the first Indian to win the Gandhi Peace Prize?

83. When was the First Five Year Plan started in India?

84. The Indian Constitution can be amended under this law. Name it.

85. Where in India will you find the rocket launching station?

86. Who was India's first woman ambassador?

87. Where in modern Pakistan did Emperor Kanishka have his capital?

88. Who administered the oath of office to Jawaharlal Nehru as the first Prime Minister of Free India?

89. Who was the first Chief Minister to be assassinated while in office?

90. Where is the seat of the Dalai Lama in India?

91. In whose honour did Emperor Akbar build Fathepur Sikri?

92. Who was Shivaji's father?

93. Which Mughal Emperor granted land in Amritsar to build the Golden Temple?

94. Which Mughal Emperor levied Jazia tax on non-Muslims?

95. How many storeys of the Qutub Minar could Qutub-ud-din Aibak complete before his death?

96. Who destroyed the famous Nalanda University?

97. Who was defeated by Babur in the First Battle of Panipat?

98. Which battle led to the establishment of the Mughal Empire in India?

99. Who built the Red Fort in Delhi?

100. Where is the mausoleum of Sher Shah Suri located?

101. In which year was Afghanistan separated from the Indian empire as a result of the treaty signed between Nadir Shah and Mohammad Shah?

102. Who carried away Shah Jahan's Peacock throne and the Kohinoor diamond to Persia?

103. Which temple did Mahmud of Ghazni plunder?

104. Where are the Cellular Jails situated?

105. Who was the Frontier Gandhi of India's struggle for Freedom?

106. Gandhiji undertook the Dandi March in 1930 to break a law? Which law was it?

107. Who was proclaimed Empress of India in 1876 when the British Crown took over the East India Company to rule India?

108. Which Indian personality was described as the 'Half naked seditious fakir' by Winston Churchill?

109. Who handed over the INA to Subhash Chandra Bose in 1943 in Singapore?

110. When was India's first pictorial postage stamp released?

111. Who founded the Rashtriya Swayemsevak Sangh (RSS) in Nagpur in 1925 ?

112. Raigarh fort in Maharashtra is associated with which historical personality?

113. In the Indian National Emblem, two animals are seen standing on the right and left sides. What are they?

114. Who was the founder of the Aligarh Muslim University?

115. Who first spread the message of Hinduism at the World Congress of Religions held at Chicago?

116. Name the place in South Africa where Gandhiji suffered solitary confinement.

117. Who wrote *Sare Jehan Se Accha*?

118. Which is the largest mosque in India?

119. Shantivana is a memorial to a former Prime Minister. Name him.

120. Under which Article of the Indian Constitution does the President declare emergency in a state.

121. Which is the world's longest Constitution?

122. Name the first state to come under President's rule?

123. Who was the first Acting President of India after the death of Zakir Husain?

124. Which Finance Minister of India presented the first budget of free India?

125. What is the minimum age for the Vice-President of India?

126. Who is the country's highest civil servant?

127. *Satyameve Jayate* is inscribed below our National Emblem. What language is it written in?

128. Name the first state that came into existence after India's Independence.

129. Which Sikh Guru was born in Patna?

130. Who was the first Indian Air Chief?

131. Who was the first Army Chief to be assassinated?

132. Who was the first Naval Chief to be dismissed from service?

133. Which is India's largest constituency in terms of voters?

134. In which year was the age limit for voting in India reduced from 21 to 18 years?

135. Which state was the first to use voting machines?

136. Who is the only Indian Prime Minister to be awarded Pakistan's highest Award 'Nishan-i-Pak'?

137. Who was the only foreign national who was awarded the Bharat Ratna?

138. Who was the leader of the Gorkha movement who survived an assassination bid in February 2001 in Darjeeling?

139. A bus service was started between two cities of India and Pakistan. Which two cities does it connect?

140. Name the constituency from which Sushma Swaraj fought Sonia Gandhi.

# Answers
## History

1. Mithila in North Bihar

2. Perfected or refined

3. Sharda

4. Bharata Muni

5. Gerek

6. Indra Sabha

7. Chandragupta Maurya

8. The Bhagavad Gita

9. Ajanta Frescos

10. Kilich Khan or Asaf Jah

11. Sapta Sindhu

12. Kashmir

13. Phoenix Farm

14. Redcliffe

15. Mahatma Gandhi

16. Maharani Gayatri Devi in Jaipur

17. A. B. Vajpayee

18. India Gate

19. Kamaladevi Chattopadhayaya

20. The Minas

21. Hawa Mahal, Jaipur

22. Kalijar in Madhya Pradesh

23. City Palace, Jaipur

24. The Stupa at Piprachiva, Bihar

25. Lothal in Gujarat

26. Vithala Complex at Hampi

27. Ramanathaswamy Temple at Rameshwaram

28. Jagannath Temple complex at Puri, Orissa

29. Kadambini Ganguly

30. Sachidanand Sinha

31. Jogindra Nath Mandal

32. Gomukh glacier in Uttar Pradesh

33. Jehangir

34. Varanasi

35. Gol Gumbaz

36. Razia Sultana

37. William Bentinck

38. At the second session of Mymensingh Suhrid Samiti Ptratapaditya Brata

39. April 1926

40. Annie Besant

41. Pune

42. Sarojini Naidu

43. Gulbadan

44. Beant Singh

45. Sawai Jai Singh II of Jaipur

46. Hanamkonda, Andhra Pradesh

47. Bangalore

48. Amber Fort, Jaipur

49. Kurnool

50. Uttaranchal

51. Bhopal Gas tragedy of 1984

52. Guwahati to Barauni in Assam

53. Bombay OffShore

54. Kandla Free Trade Zone (KAFTZ)

55. Digboi in Assam

56. Mughal emperor Shah Jahan

57. Bombay

58. Hazari Duar, the palace of the Nawab of Murshidabad

59. Jehangir

60. Rajiv Gandhi

61. Joachim and Violet Alva in the first Lok Sabha

62. Dadabhoy Nowroji

63. Qutub Sahib, spiritual heir of Moinuddin Chisti of Ajmer.

64. Prafulla Kumar Mahanta

65. Laloo Prasad Yadav

66. Clement Atlee

67. Digamber Vishnu Paluskar

68. The Greeks

69. Priyadarsi

70. Jawaharlal Nehru

71. Shah Jahan

72. Gondwanaland

73. Jainism

74. Thakkar Bapa

75. Raja Sekhra

76. Varanasi

77. Guru Tej Bahadur

78. Bal Gangadhar Tilak

79. Jatin Das

80. Lord William Bentinck

81. 1953

82. Baba Amte

83. 1962

84. Article 368

85. Sriharikota

86. Vijaylakshmi Pandit

87. Peshawar

88. Lord Mountbatten

89. Beant Singh of Punjab

90. Dharmashala, Mcleod Ganj

91. Salim Chisti

92. Shahji

93. Akbar

94. Aurangzeb

95. One

96. Bhaktiyar Khilji

97. Ibrahim Lodhi

98. Battle of Panipat

99. Shah Jahan

100. Sasaram, Bihar

101. 1739

102. Nadir Shah

103. Somnath Temple in Gujarat

104. Andaman and Nicobar Islands

105. Khan Abdul Ghaffar Khan

106. Salt Law

107. Queen Victoria

108. Gandhiji

109. Rash Behari Bose

110. 1931

111. R. K. B. Hedgewar

112. Shivaji

113. Bull and Horse

114. Sir Syed Ahmed Khan

115. Swami Vivekanda

116. Pretoria

117. Mohd Iqbal

118. Jama Masjid

119. Jawaharlal Nehru

120. Article 352

121. Indian Constitution

122. Punjab

123. V. V. Giri

124. R. K. Shankukham Chetty

125. 35 years

126. Cabinet Secretary

127. Devnagari

128. Andhra Pradesh

129. Guru Gobind Singh

130. S Mukherjee

131. Gen A.S. Vaidya

132. Vishnu Bhagat

133. Outer Delhi

134. 1989

135. Kerala

136. Morarji Desai

137. Mother Teresa

138. Subhash Ghising

139. Delhi and Lahore

140. Bellary in Karnataka

# Questions
## Science

1. Which Indian mathemetical work deals with geometry?

2. The flowering of which grass in North East India is said to indicate drought, famine or epidemic?

3. Which Coral island in the Gulf of Kutch is a protected area for green turtles?

4. In the 6$^{th}$ century, this Indian propounded the ancient Atomic theory. Name him.

5. A standard text on Ayurveda contains an oath of honesty and service to mankind similar to the Hippocratic oath. Which text is it?

6. Indian Rhinos are generally found in Assam. In which sanctuary were they recently introduced?

SCIENCE

7. Where is the Nalsarovar Bird Sanctuary located?

8. Anthropologists who discovered fossils of hominids dating back at least 14,000,000 years have named them Ramapithecus, Sugrivapithecus and Shivapithecus. Where were they discovered.

9. Which Indian breed of dog is used in hunts for killing wild boar?

10. India's major crop maize has its origin elsewhere. Name the country.

11. The word shampoo originated from a Hindi word which meant to massage the muscles to relieve fatigue. What was the word?

12. What is the full form of TRAFFIC, an international organisation which monitors trade in wildlife?

13. Who discovered the Anther Culture technique in 1967?

14. Name the person who invented the superbug - the artifical micro-organism which can digest various

petroleum componets and can clean oil spills.

15. What is the age-old art which uses essential oils from plants for healing called?

16. Where was the first bamboo tissue culture successfully produced in 1990?

17. Tetracyline, a life-saving drug was first discovered and developed by a research group in New York. Who headed the team?

18. This scientist discovered a new group of plants - Pentoxyleae - belonging to ancient times.

19. Who is the founder of Modern Astro physics?

20. Who invented the optical fibre in 1955?

21. The father of modern chemistry discovered Mecurous nitrite in 1896? Name him.

22. Name the first Indian Satellite launched in 1975.

23. Who was the first Indian in space in 1984?

SCIENCE

24. Who propounded the earliest atomic theory in the 6th century BC in his Vaisesika Sutra?

25. Name the first Atomic power station in India.

26. The first Nuclear Implosion was in Pokhran in 1974. Who was the Prime Minister when the second Implosion took place in 1998?

27. Which Indian was the first to observe spontaneous fission - splitting of a heavy nucleus on its own - in Uranium in 1940?

28. Who was the first aeronaut to make the first parachute descent in a balloon in 1889?

29. Which is the world's first Weather-Cum-Communications satellite launched in 1982?

30. Which is the country's Oldest Planetarium built in 1962?

31. The largest radio telescope in India is located in Gauribidanur, Karnataka. Who operates it?

32. Name the first Indian woman who first set foot on Antartica in 1977?

33. Who led the First Indian Expedition to Antartica in 1982?

34. Name the scientist who climbed Mt Everest and has also been to Antartica.

35. Who was the pioneer responsible for indigenous voice recording in Calcutta in 1905?

36. Who is credited with the invention of Algebra?

37. Who was the first mathematician to treat zero as a number and show its mathematical operations?

38. Who was the inventor of differential calculus long before Newton and Leibnitz?

39. Which was the scientific institution established in 1876 where C. V. Raman discovered the Raman Effect?

SCIENCE

40. Which is the only Indian fish which migrates from the sea up river to breed and then returns?

41. In January 2001, India successfully test fired this surface to surface missile. Name it.

42. Where is the oldest Dassehri mango tree found?

43. Where was the first tea estate set up by the British in 1837?

44. Which is the country's first Agricultural University set up in 1960?

45. Which is the most endangered human community in India?

46. A unique African tribe is believed to have been brought to India by the Portuguese at the end of the 17th century. Name it.

47. Which ancient Indian surgeon invented a method of stitching ruptured intestines with the mandibles of large ants?

48. The highest windmill is at an altitude of 3,353 m. Where is it?

49. Which Indian scientist demonstrated the wireless transmission before Marconi?

50. Faulty pigmentation of skin is a disease. Name it.

51. The presence of lead in drinking water can cause damage to this organ. Name it.

52. Name the disease in which the patient suffers paralysis accompanied by tremor of limbs and reduced dopamine in tissue of the brain.

53. This cancer attacks bone marrow. What is the medical term?

54. What is the treatment to remove excess fat from the body called?

55. Which chemical is used to increase the octane number of petrol?

SCIENCE

56. The smallest bone in the body is the stirrup (stapes) bone in the ear. Which is the longest?

57. Which was the first wild life sanctuary set up in India?

58. Which planet has wind speed upto 2000 km (wind speeds upto) ph?

59. The first instrument to detect earthquakes was invented in 132 AD. Name the country where it was invented.

60. After World War II, this joint military force was created by the Allies for mutual benefit. Name it.

61. Pablo Picasso was a famous sculptor and painter. Which country did he hail from?

62. What does a Lepidopterist do?

63. Which Indian bird lays the largest egg?

64. The largest tree canopy in India covers 2.1 hectares. Where do you find this 600 year-old- tree?

65. Where in India will you find the country's longest fossil woods?

66. Name the only true deer found in Kashmir?

67. Which is the largest deer found in India?

68. Which is the rarest deer found in floating habitation?

69. Where is the rare Asiatic Ass found?

70. Which is the only flying mammal?

71. Which is the longest reptile found in Nicobar Islands and Sunderbans?

72. This is the most poisonous snake found in India. Name it.

73. Where was the first white tiger captured in 1951?

74. Which is the country's only ape found in North-east India?

75. Which is the last refuge of the Asiatic Lion?

SCIENCE

76. Where is the world's largest teak tree found?

77. Name the process in which you use worms to help make compost?

78. Bhanu Tap was the name of the first solar heater devised in India. Where was it first used?

79. The first SuperComputer Cray-X MP-14 was installed in India in 1989. Where was it installed?

80. In 1983, two scientists forwarded the theory about the flipping of earth's magnetic field, i.e North becoming the South Pole and vice versa. Name the scientists.

81. Where in India will you find the hottest spring in the world?

82. Who performed the first open heart surgery in India?

83. Name the first Indian lady to acquire a degree in medicine in 1883.

84. Name the doctor who was responsible for the birth of the first Test Tube baby in India?

85. Where was the first Modern Hospital started in India in 1664?

86. Which is the most common form of cancer found in India?

87. Salim Ali received the Paul Getty Award in 1979? What was his profession?

88. Which place in India receives rainfall for over 150 days a year?

89. Name the largest Non Governmental Conservation organisation in the country.

90. Who was the first scientist to have conducted dissection of the human body?

91. Name the first person to discover the existence of male and female reproductive cells?

92. What does a taxonomist study?

SCIENCE

93. What is the study of annual rings in trees to determine dates and environmental conditions in the past, known as?

94. One branch of biology deals with the effects of extraterrestrial living organisms via probes or otherwise. What is this branch called?

95. What is the name given to the study of behaviour of animals in their natural environment?

96. A special term has been coined to describe the science of the health of travellers. Name it.

97. What is the name given to the international project which is trying to decipher the human gene code?

98. A type of white blood cell with a very large nucleus, rich in DNA, and a small amount of clear cytoplasm is found in the blood. It produces antibodies and fights diseases. Name it.

99. Which tissue of the body forms a heat insulating layer just beneath the skin?

100. Who coined the word Vitamin?.

101. Why does India celebrate February 28 each year as the National Science Day?

102. Name the vitamin whose deficiency can cause night blindness?

103. How old is our earth?

104. Who first discovered viruses causing mosaic disease in tobacco plants.

105. Which English writer bitterly attacking Darwin's theories remarked "A hen is only an egg's way of producing another egg?"

106. How much blood does an average human have in his body?

107. When man purposely selects desirable breeds of plants and animals for further propagation, the process is known as?

108. Which scientist independently arrived at the same conclusions regarding evolution as did Darwin?

109. Who discovered the remains of 'Lucy' the most famous australopithecine found in Ethopia in 1974?

110. How many species of living animals have been catalogued by biologists so far?

111. Which is the smallest warm-blooded animal in the world?

112. Which fossil organism is usually regarded as the connecting link between reptiles and birds?

113. What is Aristotle's lantern?

114. Which is the longest insect in the world?

115. Which insects are generally considered to be the loudest of all?

116. Most sharks are heavier than water. How do they prevent themselves from sinking?

117. Which is the only snake to build a nest?

118. Which is the largest living bird?

119. What are a bird's wing flight feathers called?

120. Which mammal has a natural sun-burn lotion?

121. Mammals are divided into several orders. Which order includes the most advanced mammals?

122. Where do Polar Bears live?

123. What is the name given to the pouch in which a kangaroo keeps her young baby?

124. After a forest fire, the above ground plants die. Which plants are the first to reappear?

125. Name the plant whose berries are used to make Gin?

126. Which famous biologist attenuated the germs of anthrax disease by heating them and inoculated sheep with them, thus making the sheep resistant to anthrax?

127. This person was accomplished in music, art and six languages. He left home for law school but

gained a reputation as a writer. He was also a great biologist and founded the science of morphology? Name him.

128. Which scientist first extracted 'rennet' from a calf's stomach, helping to make cheese more easily?

129. When did agriculture originate?

130. Which pesticide represents about 50 per cent of the total volume of the pesticides used in India?

131. Which animal is generally considered as the first to be domesticated by man?

132. The famous Crystal Palace, built in Hyde Park, London, to house the Great Exhibition of 1851 was inspired by a plant? Name it.

133. Which plant's seeds inspired the invention of Velcro Fastners by engineer Georges De Mestral?

134. A scientist who was colour blind was the first to describe colour blindness. Colour blindness is often named after him.

135. Living and non-living elements of an environemnt that function together as a system are known as?

136. This book published in 1859 is still regarded as one of the classics of science. All the copies of the book were snapped up on the first day of the publication. Name the book.

137. Who was the first scientist to record the electrical activity of the brain using his son as a subject?

138. What is the total amount of living material in a unit of area known as?

139. What per cent of solar energy reaching the earth's surface is converted into biomass?

140. Who wrote the monumental Principles of Geology which popularised the view that earth was more than 6,000 years old, thus laying the foundation of the theory of evolution?

141. The seeds of which tree are so uniform in weight that they were once used as standard weights by goldsmiths?

SCIENCE

142. Where in the body will you find a bundle of His?

143. Compounds released by White Blood Cells which raise the body's temperature are known as?

144. The Largest and the First Crocodile Bank was founded in 1976. Where is it located?

145. Name the largest Rookery for marine sea turtles were Olive Ridley turtles come each year to lay eggs.

146. The highest peak in the Aravali range is in Rajasthan. Name it.

147. Two streams form the Chenab river. Name them.

148. The largest telescope in Asia is located in Kavalur, Tamil Nadu. It is named after a famous Indian astrophysicist. Who was he?

149. What part of the body is affected by the AIDS virus?

150. Who invented the theory of relativity'?

151. What metal is as strong as steel but half in weight?

152. Name the first space shuttle that reached Jupiter.

153. Which part of the cocoa tree is a source of natural chocolate flavour?

154. Which is the commonly used nuclear fuel used in nuclear reactors?

155. How will you describe the shape of the earth?

156. What does 'Book Scorpions' refer to?

157. What fuel is used to run modern submarines?

158. Name the atmospheric layer damaged due to supersonic aircraft?

159. Which satellite orbits earth at low altitude?

160. Which device is used to listen to the depths of sea?

161. Who laid the foundation of space science in India?

162. Where in India was Cyclotron – the particle accelerator machine, first installed?

SCIENCE

163. Who is the inventor of dynamite and blasting gelatin?

164. Who invented the electric battery?

165. Which is the tallest flying bird?

166. Name the state with the largest coal reserve?

167. Which bird is called a snake bird?

168. Name the bird with the longest feathers?

169. Where is the headquarters of the Geological Survey of India?

170. What acid is produced when milk turns sour?

171. Which place is called the Roof of the World?

172. Where is the Temple of Emerald Buddha located?

173. Which is the biggest natural satellite in the universe?

174. Which planet has rings made up of glittering icy particles?

175. Who proposed the anti-particle theory?

176. How long does it take for the moonlight to reach earth?

177. The First Science City in India was inaugurated in 1997. Where is it located?

178. Who are the scavenger organisms of earth?

179. What is the measure of speed of ships called?

180. Which family of birds is considered the most intelligent?

181. Name the reptile which is known for its colour changing?

182. Which bird has a chisel like bill?

183. Which part of the eye perceives the image?

184. What is the literal meaning of 'Ayurveda'?

185. Which yoga can cure diseases by physical exercises?

SCIENCE

186. Whom do the 'Ayurvedic' practitioners regard as the 'God of Medicine'?

187. Who was the ancient sage who, as the legend goes, was able to regain his youth by celestial favour and after whom a popular 'Ayurvedic' tonic is named?

188. What is the name of the destructive storm that often comes at the end of the harvest season in Eastern India?

189. What did the Arabs themselves call the Indian numerals they took to the west from India and referred to as 'Arabic numerals'?

190. What was the name of the Sanskrit treatise on astronomy, which the Arabs translated and named *Sind-Hind*?

191. Who was the author of the ancient Indian theory that explained the beginning of creation as the fusion of an atom each, of earth, fire, water and air.

192. An animal species found in India is a mixture of a goat and a sheep, and belongs to neither and so has been allotted a separate genus. Name it.

193. A great eruption of lava covered parts of western India, 70 million years ago and then solidified into rock. Name the region.

194. A Buddhist philosopher wrote the *Rasa Ratnakara*. What is this text about? Who is the author?

195. Which Vedic astronomer first catalogued heavenly constellations as *Nakshatra*?

196. Name the type of falcon that lays its eggs in its own nest while most others do not bother to make their nests at all.

197. Who wrote the 5th century Indian astronomical treatise based on Greek studies and called the *Romaka Siddhanta*?

198. At what interval does the Indian lunar calendar add a leap month in order to tally with the solar calendar?

SCIENCE

199. In which forest type is the Magnolia tree found?

200. What is the name of the text in which Kapila puts forward a theory that all matter is derived from a pure primordial matrix of energy called Prakriti?

# Answers
## Science

1. Sulva Sutras

2. Bamboo

3. Bhydar

4. Kannada

5. Charaka Samhita

6. Dudhwa Wildlife Sanctuary in Uttar Pradesh

7. In Gujarat.

8. In the Shivaliks

9. Rayalseema

10. America

11. Champna

12. Trade Records Analysis of Flora and Fauna in Commerce

13. S. C. Maheswari and Sipra Mukherjee

14. Ananda M. Chakraborty

15. Aromatherepy

16. National Chemical Laboratory, Pune

17. Dr. Yellapragada Subbarow.

18. Birbal Sahni

19. Meghnad Saha

20. Narinder Kapary

21. Prafulla Chandra Ray

22. Aryabhatta

23. Squadron Leader Rakesh Sharma

24. Kanada

25. Tarapore Power Station near Mumbai

26. Atal Behari Vajpayee

27. Syama Das Chatterjee

28. Ramchunder Chatterjee

29. INSAT (I A)

30. The Birla Planetarium in Kolkata

31. The Indian Institute of Astrophysics and the Raman Research Institute

32. Mehar H. Moos

33. Dr S. Z. Qasim

34. Dr C. P. Vohra

35. Hemchandra Bose

36. Aryabhatta

37. Brahmagupta

38. Bhaskara

39. Indian Association for the Cultivation of Science in Calcutta

40. Hilsa

41. Agni II

42. The mother tree is found in Maliahabad, Lucknow

43. Chubwa, Dibrugarh, Assam

44. Govind Ballabh Pant University, Pantnagar, Nainital

45. The Great Andamanese Shompen and Onge living in Andaman and Nicobar islands.

46. The Siddis.

47. Susruta

48. Choglamsar at Leh, J & K

49. Jagdish Chander Bose

50. Leukoderma

51. Kidneys

52. Parkinson's disease

53. Leukaemia

54. Lipolysis

55. Tetraethyl lead

56. Femur

57. Jim Corbett National Park

58. Neptune

59. China

60. NATO

61. Spain

62. Study butterflies

63. Sarus Crane

64. Thimmamma Marrimanu village in Anantpur district of Andhra Pradesh

65. Tiruvakkarai National Park, Pondicherry

66. Hangul

67. Sambhar

68. Sangai or Manipur brow antlered deer in Manipur

69. Little Rann of Kutch

70. Bat

71. Reticulated Python

72. Banded Krait

73. Rewa, Madhya Pradesh

74. Hoolock Gibbon

75. Gir in Gujarat

76. Malayattur Forest Division in Kerala

77. Vermicomposting

78. Almora, Uttar Pradesh

79. National Centre for Medium Range weather forecasting

80. J. G. Negi and R. R. Tewari

81. Vashist Springs near Manali, Himachal Pradesh

82. D. N. Gopinath and R. H. Betts of Christian Medical College Hospital, Vellore.

83. Anandibai Joshi

84. Dr. Indira Hinduja

85. At Fort St. George, Madras

86. Oral Cancer

87. Omithelogy (Ornithology)

88. Mawsynaram

89. World Wide Fund for Nature (WWF)

90. Alcmaeon, Greek physican flourished around 520 BC

SCIENCE

91. Hippocrates

92. Classification of organisms

93. Dendrochronology

94. Space biology

95. Ethology

96. Emporiatrics

97. The Human Genome Code

98. Lymphocyte

99. Adipose tissue

100. Funk, an American biochemist.

101. This is in memory of scientist C. V. Raman who discovered the Raman effect on this day

102. Vitamin A

103. 4.6 billion years

104. Beijerinck, a Dutch Microbiologist

105. Samuel Butler

106. Four Litres

107. Artifical Selection

108. Alfred Russel Wallace

109. Donald Johanson

110. 1,2000,000 and about 10,000 new animal species are being discovered each year

111. Bee Humming bird of Cuba weighs just 2 gms

112. Archaeopteryx

113. Five teeth of a sea urchin are so arranged that it looks like a lantern and works like a food shredder

114. The females of the tropical stick insect have been measured upto 330 mm

115. Male cicadas

116. By movement through the water

117. King Cobra

118. Ostrich

119. Remiges

120. Hippopotamus

121. Primates

122. Only in the North Pole

123. Marsupium

124. Ferns as their underground rhizomes develop new leaves

125. Juniperius (its blue-black berries are used to flavour gin)

126. Louis Pasteur

127. Johann Wolfgang Goethe

128. Christian Hansen

129. 7,000-13000 years ago

130. BHC

131. The Dog

132. Water Lily

133. Burdock Seeds have minute hooks

134. John Dalton

135. Ecosystem

136. Origin of Species

137. Hans Berger invented this technique now known as electroencephalography (EEG)

138. Biomass

139. 50 per cent

140. Sir Charles Lyall

141. Carob, an evergreen tree found in Southern Europe and the Middle East. The weight of one seed is known as carat

142. In the heart. This is a group of special muscle fibres found in the heart which transmits electrical impulses. William His Jr was the first to describe this

143. Pyrogens

144. Madras Crocodile Bank, Madras

145. Gahir Matha region of Orissa

146. Gurushikhar peak

147. Chandra and Bhaga

148. Dr. Vaina Bappu.

149. The immune system

150. Albert Einstein

151. Titanium

152. Pioneer-10

153. Seeds

154. Plutonium

155. Geoid

156. False spider

157. Nuclear fuel

158. Ozone layer

159. Spy Satellite

160. Hydrophone

161. Vikram Sarabhai

162. Calcutta

163. Alfred Nobel

164. Alexantro Volta

165. Sarus Crane

SCIENCE

166. Bihar

167. Darter

168. Phoenix fowl

169. Calcutta

170. Lactic acid

171. Plateau of Tibet

172. Bangkok

173. Ganymede

174. Saturn

175. P.A.M. Dirac

176. Less than 60 seconds

177. Kolkata

178. Bacteria & Fungi

179. Knot

180. Crows

181. Chameleon

182. Woodpecker

183. Retina

184. 'Science of Life'

185. Hatha Yoga

186. Dhanwantari

187. Chyavana

188. Kal-Baisakhi

189. Hindsa

190. The Brahma Gupta Siddhanta

191. Kanada

192. The bharal

193. The Deccan Trap

194. Text on alchemy; Nagarjuna

195. Gargeya

196. The Red Headed Merlin or *turmti* (Falco chiquera)

197. Srisena

198. At thirty months' interval

199. Wet temperate forest

200. The Sankhya Sutra

# Questions
## Sports

1. Which ancient system of physical culture was revived by Balambhatta Dada Deodhar in the early 19th century?

2. Which was the first Indian badminton player to reach the finals of the All England Championship in 1947?

3. K. D. Jadhav was the first Indian to win an individual medal (bronze) at any Olympics. What event did he participate in?

4. The world's oldest recognised Polo Club is in Calcutta. What is its name?

5. A popular cricketer of Sri Lanka owns a restaurant Curry Leaves in Colombo. Who is this sportsman?

6. What is the ball used in ice-hockey called ?

SPORTS

7. What is brain bucket in cricket slang?

8. Which international game was actually invented in Jabalpur?

9. Ludo is actually derived from this ancient Indian board game.

10. How many wooden pieces do you see on a cricket field?

11. In the 99-2000 tour of Australia, which Indian cricketer had the dubious distinction of four first ball ducks?

12. Which bird's feathers are used to make a shuttlecock?

13. Who is the Indian cricketer to have played the maximum number of one-day internationals?

14. Which cricketer got all 10 wickets in one innings against Pakistan?

15. Who is the first Indian to bat with a helmet on?

16. Who is the youngest batsman to score four centuries?

17. How many dimples will you find in a golf ball?

18. The daughter of a famous cricketer became the first woman cricket commentator of India. Name her.

19. Name the first woman horse trainer in India.

20. Which is the largest stadium in the world?

21. Name the largest indoor stadium in the country.

22. Name the sports person who represented India in six Olympics.

23. Which sport has the maximum number of team members (110)?

24. The largest sports trophy in India is 6 ft tall. Name it.

25. Two sportsmen have received both the Arjuna Award and Dronacharya Award for being the best

players and the coach in their field. Name them.

26. The country's first ski club was opened in 1972. Where was it set up?

27. Name the sportswoman who took the maximun number of golds in the 1984 Asian games.

28. Which Badminton player was the first to win the Asian Championship in 1965?

29. Name the first Badminton Academy opened by a former national champion in 1994.

30. Name the first Indian to win the World Amateur Championship in Billiards in 1958.

31. Name the sportsman who won the world professional Billiards championship in 1992.

32. Name the only Indian to win the World Chess Title in 2000.

33. What was the name given to Chess in Ancient India?

34. Who was the first Indian woman to scale Mt Everest in 1984?

35. One Indian woman has climbed the Mt Everest twice. Name her.

36. A group of 10 Sappers led by Col T. P. Chowdhury circumnavigated in a fibre glass yacht. Name the yacht.

37. Which cricketer said, "I wanted to be a bus driver, wonder what got me into cricket?"

38. A life ban on playing cricket has been imposed on this cricketer following allegations of match fixing. Name him.

39. The Subroto Cup is associated with which game?

40. Who was the first cricketer to score a hattrick in a one day International cricket match?

41. What is the percentage of gold present in an Olympic gold medal?

SPORTS

42. Which sport makes use of all the body muscles?

43. Which cricket stadium has hosted the maximum number of one day International cricket matches?

44. Name the first cricketer to score 10,000 runs, play 100 test matches, and take 100 test catches?

45. How many squares will you find in a chess board?

46. Which is the most mobile chess piece?

47. Which hunting instrument appeared as part of the logo of the 2000 Sydney Olympic games?

48. Who was the youngest captain of the Indian Cricket Team?

49. Name the first Indian to win the Grand Slam Tennis Title.

50. Which Tennis player is nicknamed "Stilt from split?"

51. Which is the fastest swimming stroke?

52. What is the minimum age for participating in the Olympics?

53. The Ranji Trophy is named after this famous Indian cricketer. Name him.

54. In which sport is a 10 yard cloth folded six times worn by participants?

55. Which country has won the maximum number of gold medals in hockey?

56. Which Tennis tournament starts six Mondays back from the first Monday of August?

57. Name the first sport played in outer space.

58. In Archery, what colour is in the centre of the target?

59. Under whose captaincy did Sachin Tendulkar make his debut?

60. Name one Indian Cricketer who married dancer Dona Ray.

SPORTS

61. This Indian cricketer cried during a BBC interview when questioned about the match fixing allegations against him. Name him.

62. Which former Pakistani batsman was nicknamed 'Mr Majestic'?

63. After India's Independence, who was the captain of the first Pakistani Cricket team to visit India?

64. Which Pakistani cricketer called his autobiography Zed?

65. Which Indian cricketer is associated with the music Album 'Rest Day'?

66. Name the cricketer who has turned into a popular TV star?

67. Who is the only International Umpire who was given honorary Life Membership of MCC?

68. The Caribbean Island of St Vincent issued a stamp in honour of this Indian cricketer. Name him.

69. What is the name of the autobiography of Kapil Dev?

70. When was the first Vintage car rally held in India?

71. Rover's Cup is associated with which sport?

72. When did India win the first Polo World Cup?

73. Name the first Indian to win the British Formula 3 Circuit in 1999.

74. Which is the oldest swimming club in India?

75. Which Indian tennis player has won "Hall of Fame" Teams tournament in USA thrice?

76. India scored the highest of 373 for 6 in 50 overs at Taunton in 1999. Which country were they playing against?

77. What sport was Guru Hanuman associated with?

78. In which sport did Leander Paes's father Vece Paes, represent India at the international level?

79. On whose birthday is the National Sports Day celebrated?

80. India's largest sports complex is named after this personality. Name him.

81. Name the first woman jockey of India who later chose to teach in a primary school.

82. With which sport is the Prime Minister's official residence associated?

83. Which Indian won the first Asian Snooker Championship?

84. The Indian Cricket team was on a tour abroad when Indira Gandhi was assassinated. Name the country.

85. Milkha Singh broke the world record of a 400 mt event here. Name the city.

86. Which Indian participated in the national Veteran Athletic Championship at the age of 100?

87. In which track and field event is the Western Roll method used?

88. Which British Prime Minister played first-class cricket?

89. In which game did Aparna Popat win a Silver medal at the 1998 Commonwealth Games?

90. Who is the youngest Indian Chess player to have won the International Master title?

91. Rajesh Chauhan took 132 minutes to make 9 runs. Where was this world record made?

92. Where is the world's highest cricket ground?

93. How many double centuries did cricketer Don Bradman score in his Test career?

94. How many rings are there in the top row of the Olympic flag?

95. Who won a gold medal in the 50 km walk at Asiad 51 in Delhi?

SPORTS

96. Who won the first archery medal for India in the 1988 Asia Cup?

97. Which Ranji player from Hyderabad, besides Azharuddin, became a test captain?

98. Cricket bats are made from the wood of this tree. Name it.

99. Who was the first Indian woman to go into space?

100. At which Olympic Game was *kabaddi* first demonstrated?

101. What is the name by which a popular board game, called *pallanguli* in Tamil is referred to in other parts of India?

102. In Himachal Pradesh a game of archery is played by villages as a team against one another. This game dates back to the time of the *Mahabharata*. Name the game.

103. What is the present name of the Indian sport originally called *rathera*, as it was played on *raths* or chariots.

104. In the *Inbuan* wrestling style, the wrestler has to pull up his opponent rather than pin him down. Where does this style belong?

105. The British officers made a sport out of the elements of the first Indian War of Independence in 1857 by a board game. Name it.

106. Which Buddhist monk is believed to have introduced the martial art *kalaripayattu* to China and Japan?

107. In an Indian sport called *Ke nang huan* the men fight wild pigs. Name the place this sport belongs to.

108. In which state of eastern India is *Yubee – lakpee* a variation on rugby, played, where the ball is usually a well greased coconut?

109. Which Indian cricketer played Test cricket for both England and India?

110. Who instituted the first football national championship in India?

# Answers
## Sports

1. Mallakhamb (gymnasts pole)

2. Vijay Madgavkar

3. Wrestling

4. Calcutta Club

5. Aravinda De Silva

6. Puck

7. Helmet

8. Snooker

9. Pachisi

10. Twelve

11. Ajit Agarkar

SPORTS

12. Goose

13. Mohd. Azharuddin

14. Anil Kumble

15. Mohinder Amarnath

16. Kapil Dev

17. 400

18. Chandra Nayadu

19. Arti Doctor

20. Yuba Bharati (Salt Lake) Calcutta

21. Indira Gandhi Indoor Stadium, New Delhi

22. R. K. Randhir Singh

23. Snake boat races held Onam in Kerala

24. Kolanka Cup for Polo

25. Syed Nayeemuddin and A Ramana Rao

26. Gulmarg, Kashmir

27. P. T. Usha

28. Dinesh Khanna

29. Prakash Padukone Badminton Academy in Bangalore

30. Wilson Jones

31. Geet Sethi

32. Vishwanathan Anand

33. Chaturanga

34. Bachendri Pal

35. Santosh Yadav

36. Trishna

37. Kapil Dev

38. Mohd Azharuddin

SPORTS

39. Football

40. Chetan Sharma

41. 5.2 per cent

42. Swimming

43. Sharjah Cricket Stadium

44. Sunil Gavaskar

45. 64

46. Queen

47. Boomerang

48. M. A. K. Pataudi

49. Mahesh Bhupati

50. Govan Ivanesic

51. Freestyle

52. No age limit

53. K. S. Ranjit Singh

54. Sumo Wrestling

55. India

56. Wimbeldon

57. Chess

58. Golden

59. Kapil Dev

60. Saurav Ganguly

61. Kapil Dev

62. Majid Khan

63. A. H. Kardar

64. Zaheer Abbas

65. Sanjay Manjerekar

66. Salil Ankola

SPORTS

67. Dickie Bird

68. Sunil Gavaskar

69. By God's Decree

70. 1964

71. Football

72. 1957

73. Narain Karthikeyan

74. Calcutta Swimming Club

75. Vijay Amritraj

76. Sri Lanka

77. Wrestling

78. Hockey

79. Dhyan Chand

80. Subhas Chandra Bose

81. Ayesha Captain

82. Horse Race

83. Yasin Merchant

84. Pakistan

85. Rome

86. Kodanda Ramaiah

87. High Jump

88. Alec Douglas Home

89. Badmintion

90. Vishwanathan Anand

91. Ahmedabad

92. Chail, Himachal Pradesh

93. 12

94. Three

SPORTS

95. Bakhtawar Singh

96. Shyam Lal

97. Asif Iqbal

98. Willow

99. Kalpana Chawla

100. Berlin Olympics 1936

101. Mancala

102. Thoda

103. Kho-kho

104. Mizoram

105. Officers and Sepoys

106. Bodhi – Dharma

107. Nicobar Islands

108. Manipur

109. Iftikar Ali Khan, Nawab of Pataudi

110. Sir Mortimer Durand in 183

# Questions
## Miscellanesous

1. Where was the first lift installed in Calcutta?

2. The first train journey began in India in the year 1853. About 400 passengers boarded the train. Which two stations did it connect?

3. Ancient Aryans called river Indus by another name. What was it?

4. The longest human-powered boats in the world are used during a festival in India. Name the festival.

5. The famous Battle of Longwalla of the 1971 Indo Pak War was the basis of this film. Name it.

6. India's only handwritten newspaper started in 1969 and it still exists. Name the paper.

MISCELLANEOUS

7. Which is the only newspaper simultaneously published from Delhi, Mumbai and London?

8. Name the first woman cartoonist of India whose cartoon strip Suki first appeared in Sunday Observer in 1982.

9. Which is India's highest selling Daily?

10. From where was the first radio broadcast made in 1921?

11. Which was the first telefilm shown on Doordarshan?

12. Name the first and longest soap opera serial shown on Indian television?

13. Which was the first newspaper in India?

14. What is an extrovert personality in Yogic terms called?

15. A South Indian Brahmin founded a royal dynasty in South East Asia. Name this country.

16. Members of this North Indian community are traditionally forbidden to spend more than Rs 13 on a wedding. Name the community.

17. In Ladakh, the bark of a tree is used in preparation of tea. The seeds of this tree are highly poisonous. Name the tree.

18. An outstanding physicist started his career in the Financial Civil Service. Who was he?

19. Which profession was the first to wear Levi's Jeans?

20. Which is the world's largest moped manufacturer?

21. A range of snacks manufactured in India are known after places. Name the company.

22. Well-known scriptwriter Javed Akhtar is associated with a pen brand. Name it.

23. An upmarket perfume was recently launched with this line: *Rahe ne Rahe Hum, Mehaka Karenge.* It is named after a world famous Indian. Name her.

24. Nobel Laureate Amartya Sen set up a trust with part of the Nobel Prize money. What is this trust?

25. Which was the first Indian company to have been listed in the New York Stock Exchange?

26. Which Indian bank made history for selling *Prasad* to devotees at a temple?

27. Which is India's largest manufacturer of herbal products?

28. Which watch does Cindy Crawford endorse?

29. Which airline has the maximum number of aircraft?

30. The McDonald chain serves only one brand of liquid. What is it?

31. Only one Asian company figures in the 1999 list of 100 top brands in the world. What company is it?

32. SQ is the code for a foreign airline. Name it.

33. The busiest international airport caters to over 40 million passengers each year. Name it.

34. The world's largest shopping centre is equal to about 90 football fields. Where is it?

35. Name the person who drafted the original Indian Penal Code in 1861.

36. Where is the Sathya Sai Baba's main ashram located?

37. Male is the capital of Maldives. Can you name the currency?

38. This US state was bought by the US from Russia for 7.2 million dollars. Name the state.

39. Since 1945, how many wars have been fought in the world?

40. Which commemorative monument in India carries the maximum number of names of soldiers who died fighting?

MISCELLANEOUS

41. Which is the world's longest river bridge?

42. Which is the Angor Wat of India which houses ruins of 30 Jain Temples?

43. Name the busiest bridge of the world which carries more than 60,000 vehicles every day.

44. Name the largest Residential building in India.

45. Sulabh Shauchalaya is a very popular community toilet for the poor in India. Who is the man behind this project?

46. Kalparkisha is another name for this most useful tree in India. Name it.

47. Which is India's most exported medicinal plant?

48. Where is Asia's largest fruit and vegetable market located?

49. Which is the state with the maximum number of tractors?

50. Who was the first Army chief to die in harness?

51. Where is the world's highest battle ground?

52. Where can you find the world's largest chandeliers, each weighing 3 tons?

53. The world's largest cannon on wheels is at Jaipur. What is it called?

54. Which college in India has produced 6 Defence Chiefs of India and two Air Chiefs of Pakistan?

55. Where is the oldest slide for children located?

56. The largest reward offered by a government was for the capture of this criminal. Name him.

57. The first Chief Minister to marry in office belonged to one of the states of North East. Name him.

58. Name the first couple in the Lok Sabha

59. Who was the first non-white to become a member of the British House of Commons?

60. The *Phoolwalon ki Sair* is an annual fair held at Qutub Minar in Delhi. It is held at whose grave?

MISCELLANEOUS

61. The first open prison was established in Rajasthan in 1956. Where is it?

62. Which was the first TV advertisment in 1976?

63. Where in India will you find the largest film archives?

64. The First Railway Museum of the country has a star exhibition - Fairy Queen. Where is it located?

65. Who was the youngest woman pilot to command a jet aircraft?

66. The First Stamp of Independent India was first minted in November 1947. What was inscribed on the stamp?

67. The first STD connection in India connected these two cities of North India. Name them.

68. Which is the largest Open University in India?

69. Where was the first Medical College set up in India?

70. The world's largest mosquito net can accommodate upto 10,000 people. Where is it located?

71. The first batch of women was inducted in the Army in 1993. How many women were in the batch?

72. Which Indian Industrialist who flew the first domestic flight from Karachi to Bombay, was given the honorary rank of Air Vice Marshal?

73. Which Indian University has a room where Lord Mountbatten proposed to Edwina, later his wife?

74. A small land link connects the middle of West Bengal to its southern sector. What is it called?

75. Who was the first woman president of the UN General Assembly in 1953?

76. Into how many Indian states does the Thar Desert spread?

77. Which is the biggest chain of retail Bookshops in India?

78. Who was the first professional woman pilot in the world?

79. When was the National Commission for Woman Act passed?

80. Name the organisation which was started by trade union leader Ela Bhatt in 1972.

81. Name the national body of Women Journalists.

82. Who was the first woman Justice of the Supreme Court?

83. Name the longest serving Chairman (53 years) of any business organisation.

84. The first Bank was established in India in 1770. What was it called?

85. When was the first Rupiya issued in India by Sher Shah Suri?

86. Which is India's largest seafood exporting town?

87. Name the largest selling Cigarette brand in India.

88. Which company produces the largest number of telephone instruments in the country?

89. Name the country's biggest hotel chain.

90. Which was the country's first five star hotel?

91. Where in India will you find India's largest jewellery mart?

92. Which was the first tea company to commercialise tea in 1856?

93. In whose memory was the first commemorative stamp issued in 1964?

94. In 1975, India exported cars for the first time? Which car was it?

95. Which was the first ice cream factory set up in India in 1948?

96. Name the first cigarette company set up in India in 1910.

97. Who is the first champagne manufacturer of India?

MISCELLANEOUS

98. Which is the largest scooter manufacturing company of India?

99. Name the first Indian Company to get an ISO 9000?

100. Which company in India produces the largest number of bicycles?

101. What is the word *Dum Pukht* associated with?

102. Which is the country's largest car manufacturer?

103. Name the largest children's store in the world.

104. Which is the largest detergent manufacturer of India?

105. Name the state with the maximum number of taxpayers.

106. Who is the world's largest employer?

107. Name the first Indian Public Sector undertaking to turn private.

108. Name the company with maximum shareholders.

109. Who is the only Finance Minister to have presented the Union Budget three times in a row?

110. Which is India's largest power station?

111. Where were the first incandescent lamps produced in India in 1932?

112. Name the largest petro chemical company of India.

113. Which is the largest producer and exporter of steel in India?

114. Name the first factory to manufacture dry batteries in India.

115. Which Indian magician is the only one to have been honoured with a Padmashri?

116. Name the architects behind the restoration of the Neemrana Fort in Rajasthan.

117. Who was the first woman Prime Minister in the world?

MISCELLANEOUS

118. Who was the leader who left politics and returned to Pondicherry to set up an Ashram?

119. What is the name given to an Agreement to suspend hostilities in order to negotiate for peace?

120. Which tax is levied and collected by the Union but wholly assigned to the states?

121. What is the name given to a narrow strip of land seperating two seas called?

122. Name the two celebrities who received the Bharat Ratna in 2001.

123. Where is the world's longest glacier situated?

124. Which state has the longest coastline (1600 km)?

125. Name the largest Delta in the world.

126. Where is the largest cave in India?

127. The world's second longest beach is in India. Name it.

128. Which polymer is widely used for making bullet proof materials?

129. In which state is it legal to have more than one living wife?

130. Who won the 1994 Grammy Award in the World Music category?

131. Which Indian was the first to receive the Oscar for the film Gandhi?

132. Who won the prize for deciphering the language of bees in 1973?

133. Where in India will you find the relic of a hair of Prophet Mohammad?

134. Who is the only person in the world who can calculate faster than the computer?

135. Where in India will you find the oldest naturally preserved human body?

136. Name India's one billionth baby.

MISCELLANEOUS

137. Where is the Pink City located?

138. The Chilka Lake is a famous wetland for migratory birds. Where is it located?

139. Which is the most multilingual city of the world?

140. Which state is called the "Tea Garden"?

141. When is the Human Rights Day observed?

142. Name the Airline which has the largest passenger carrying capacity?

143. Which is the most popular fruit in the world?

144. Quantas Airlines belongs to which country?

145. Who built the Eiffel Tower in 1889?

146. Which country is the largest producer of eggs in the world?

147. Where was the Statute of Liberty of New York actually made?

148. Which country used coins made of salt as currency?

149. India's 100 rupee note is signed by which civil servant?

150. Which is the largest Nationalised Bank in India?

151. What is the term fourth estate used for ?

152. When was the Reserve Bank of India established?

153. Name the first woman Mayor of Bombay?

154. What is the full form of CRY?

155. Which National Park has the largest number of tigers?

156. How many carats are there in pure gold?

157. What is India's external Intelligence agency called?

158. Rajiv Gandhi was an employee of which Airline?

159. In which year was the sari introduced as a uniform for Indian Airlines airhostesses?

MISCELLANEOUS

160. Celebrated Odissi dancer Protima Bedi died in a landslide accident during a pilgrimage trip. Where was she going?

161. Which is India's first news agency?

162. Which country manufactured the Titanic, a ship that was never to sink, but which sank on its maiden trip from London to New York?

163. What is a person who compiles a dictionary called?

164. Who made the first computer in 1941?

165. Who invented the celluloid film?

166. Where in India is the world's largest CTC tea auction centre located?

167. In 1944, Subhash Chandra Bose first hoisted the flag of the Indian National Army in North-east India. Name the place.

168. The National Geographic has described this state as one of the must see destinations in the world. Name it.

169. Which city is known as the "Manchester of South India"?

170. Name this erstwhile Maharani who disowned her son who was a former union minister.

171. Which island in Gujarat was an erstwhile Portuguese colony?

172. The Hindustan-Tibet road was built nearly 150 years ago to connect some areas of Himachal? Who was responsible for its construction?

173. Which town in Gujarat was totally destroyed during the January 2001 earthquake?

174. Name the luxury train that tours Gujarat in royal style.

175. Who is the only personality to have won the Oscar award 32 times?

176. Where in India will you find the 'open air art gallery of Rajasthan'?

177. Which field is Ritu Kumar associated with?

178. Name the institute in Bhopal which is involved in the preservation of our cultural heritage.

179. Which university was started by Rabindranath Tagore?

180. Name the designer of the international commune at Auroville, Pondicherry.

181. Raja Ravi Varma was a celebrated Indian painter. He spent most of his life in Baroda but which state did he belong to?

182. Lord Shiva is also called Nataraja. What does it mean?

183. Name the dance form where men paint their faces and dance with masks on.

184. What is pietra dura associated with?

185. Where is the biggest rose garden of Asia located?

186. Where in India will you find the space Application Centre?

187. Which rive is shared by India and Pakistan?

188. A Botanical garden called Company Bagh is 175 years old. Where is it located?

189. Name India's most advanced satellite launched in 1999?

190. Sarangi is similar to this musical instrument of the west. Name it.

191. Where is the Birbal Sahni Institute of Palaeobotany located?

192. Which plant is named after the founder of Singapore?

193. This train is declared a UN World Heritage object. Name it.

194. Some animals pass the hot summer in a torpid condition, without moving or eating anything. What is this phenomena called?

195. An imposing but incomplete temple near Bhopal is believed to have been built by Raja Bhoj in one day. Name the temple.

196. Sweat glands, tear glands and mam mary glands are examples of this gland.

197. Name the only Chief Minister of an Indian state who is a Kathak student?

198. Name the recent movie in which the trauma of Partition was depicted.

199. Name the former Chief Minister of Tamil Nadu who was arrested and later released by Chief Minister Jayalalitha.

200. Name the hotel in which Pakistan's President Mushraff stayed during his visit to Agra.

# Answers
## Miscellanesous

1. In Raj Bhavan

2. Bori Bunder and Thane in Maharastra.

3. Sindhu

4. Onam

5. Border

6. Chinese Newspaper

7. The Asian Age

8. Manjula Padmanabhan

9. Malyalam Manorama

10. *The Times of India* Office, Bombay

11. Satyajit Ray's film *Sadgati*

MISCELLANEOUS

12. Hum Log

13. The Bengal Gazette

14. Bahir Mukha

15. Kampuchea

16. Namdhari Sikhs

17. Yew (Taxus baccata)

18. C. V. Raman.

19. Miners

20. TVS

21. Britannia

22. Rotomac fighter

23. Lata Mangeshkar

24. Pratichi Trust

25. ICICI

26. The Bank of Andhra at Tirupati

27. Dabur

28. Omega

29. British Airways

30. Coke

31. Sony

32. Singapore Airlines

33. Heathrow

34. West Edmonton Mall, Alberta, Canada.

35. Thomas Babington Macaulay

36. Puttaparthi, Karnataka

37. Rufiyaa

38. Alaska

39. Over 150 wars

MISCELLANEOUS

40. India Gate, New Delhi

41. Mahatma Gandhi Setu, Bihar

42. Deogarh and Chanderi forts on Betwa River in Uttar Pradesh

43. Howrah Bridge, Calcutta

44. Rashtrapati Bhawan, New Delhi

45. Bindeshwar Pathak

46. Coconut tree

47. Isabagol (Psyllium)

48. New Subzi Mandi, Azadpur, New Delhi

49. Punjab

50. Gen B. C. Joshi

51. Siachin, Ladakh (J&K)

52. Durbar Hall of Gwalior Royal Palace

53. Jai Vana

54. Rashtriya Indian Miliatary College (RIMC) Dehradun

55. Mahabalipuram, Tamil Nadu

56. Veerapan, Sandalwood smuggler and fugitive

57. Joachim and Violet Alva in the first Lok Sabha

58. Dadabhoy Nowroji

59. Qutub Sahib, spritual heir of Moinuddin Chisti of Ajmer

60. Prafulla Kumar Mahanta

61. Jaipur

62. Gwalior Suiting

63. National Film Archives at Pune

64. Delhi

65. Nivedita Bhasin.

## MISCELLANEOUS

66. Jai Hind

67. Lucknow and Kanpur

68. The Indira Gandhi National Open University.

69. Calcutta

70. Osho Ashram, Pune

71. 25

72. J. R. D. Tata

73. Delhi University

74. The Farakka Barrage

75. Vijaylakshmi Pandit

76. Four

77. A. H. Wheeler

78. Durba Banerjee

79. August 1990

80. SEWA (Self-Employed Women's Association)

81. Indian Women's Press Corps (IWPC)

82. Fatima Beevi

83. J. R. D. Tata

84. Bank of Hindustan in Calcutta

85. 1542

86. Veraval, Junagarh, Gujarat

87. Wills Navy Cut

88. Bharati Telcom

89. Indian Hotels

90. Taj Mahal Hotel, Mumbai

91. Zaveri Bazar, Mumbai

92. Alubari Tea Estate, Assam

93. Jawaharlal Nehru

MISCELLANEOUS

94. Ambassador

95. Joy Ice Cream Company at Bombay

96. Imperial Tobacco Company (ITC)

97. Shyam Chougule's Champagne India, Maharashtra

98. Bajaj Auto

99. Sundaram partners of Suresh Krishna (orginally the TVS group)

100. Hero Cycles

101. Food. It is a form of Mughlai cuisine

102. Maruti Udyog Limited

103. Big Kids Kemp, Bangalore

104. Hindustan Lever

105. Maharashtra

106. Indian Railways

107. Maruti Udyog Ltd

108. Reliance

109. Manmohan Singh

110. Korba Thermal Power Station, Bilaspur, Uttar Pradesh

111. Bengal Electric Lamps Works Ltd

112. Reliance Petrochemicals

113. Steel Authority of India

114. Eveready Co. at their factory in Kolkata

115. P. C. Sorkar Sr.

116. Aman Nath and Francis Wacziarag

117. Srimavo Bandaranaike of Sri Lanka

118. Aurobindo Ghosh

119. Armistice

MISCELLANEOUS

120. Taxes on Railway freight

121. Isthmus

122. Lata Mangeshkar and Bismillah Khan

123. Siachen

124. Gujarat

125. Sunderbans in West Bengal

126. Amarnath Cave in Jammu and Kashmir

127. Marina Beach, Chennai

128. Polycarbonates

129. Goa

130. Vishnu Mohan Bhatt

131. Bhanu Athaya

132. Karl Von Frisch

133. Hazratbal shrine, Kashmir

134. Shakuntala Devi

135. 400 year-old body of St Francis at Bom Jesu Basillica in Goa

136. Astha

137. Jaipur in Rajasthan

138. Orissa

139. Hongkong

140. Assam

141. December 10

142. United Airline, USA

143. Orange

144. Australia

145. Gustave Eiffel

146. China

MISCELLANEOUS

147. France

148. China

149. Governor of the Reserve Bank of India

150. Bank of India

151. Press

152. 1935

153. Sulochna Modi

154. Child Relief and You

155. Kanha National Park, Madhya Pradesh

156. 24

157. Research and Analysis Wing (RAW)

158. Indian Airlines

159. 1960

160. Kailash-Mansarovar in Tibet

161. Press Trust of India (PTI)

162. UK

163. Lexicographer

164. Howard Aiken

165. George Eastman

166. Guwahati

167. Moirang, Manipur

168. Kerala

169. Coimbatore

170. Late Maharani Vijayraje Scindia of Gwalior

171. Diu

172. Lord Dalhousie

173. Bhuj

174. Royal Orient

MISCELLANEOUS

175. Walt Disney

176. Shekhawati in Rajasthan

177. Fashion

178. Rabindra Bhawan

179. Shantiniketan

180. Roger Anger

181. Kerala

182. King of Dance

183. Kathakali

184. Mughal art of using precious and semi precious stones on marble

185. Chandigarh

186. Ahmedabad

187. Indus

188. Saharanpur

189. INSAT 2E

190. Violin

191. Lucknow

192. Rafflesia

193. Darjeeling's Toy Train

194. Aestivation

195. Bhojpur

196. Exocrine glands

197. Farooq Abdullah of J & K

198. Gadar

199. M. Karunanidhi

200. Jaypee Palace

Lightning Source UK Ltd.
Milton Keynes UK
UKHW022005091220
374896UK00010B/773